Our Muscles Are Used Everyday

Copyright © 2019 by Omar Lee

Omar Lee Publishing LLC

Illustrations by Ambrosius Yunias © 2019

Songs by Blessing Mokoena © 2019

**Songs available by email. Email: omarleepublishing@gmail.com

Dad and Ma,

Thank you for sharing your love, protection, care, and
kindness. I love and respect you both deeply.

Love Omar

THE CATZ IN T-TYME

HOW DO WE USE OUR MUSCLES EVERYDAY

Our muscles are used for pulling, pushing, turning, and twisting movements each and every day.

In fact, we have nearly 630 muscles in our body that we use for work or play.

Our abdominal muscles are used for bending, leaning, and swaying movements every day.

Your abdominal muscles are located just above your belly. Can you locate your abdominal muscles?

We can also use our abdominal muscles for play!
Stretching from side to side before a game of tag or
participating in a "sit-up" relay race are two ways we
use our abdominal muscles for play.

Our bicep muscles are used for pulling movements every day. For instance, such movements happen when we pick up our shoes and then put them on. Our bicep muscles are located at the top of our arms. Can you point to your bicep muscles? List other ways we can use our bicep muscles every day.

1...
2...
3...

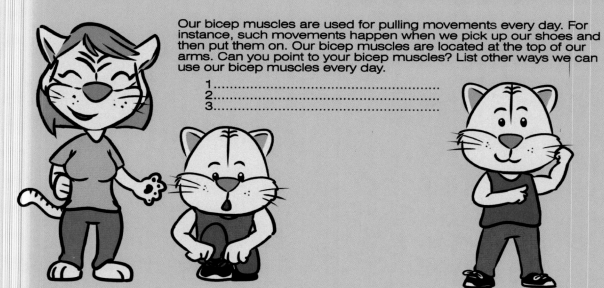

THE CATZ IN T-TYME

HOW DO WE USE OUR MUSCLES EVERYDAY

WE CAN ALSO USE OUR
BICEP MUSCLES FOR PLAY.
A GAME OF JUMP ROPE
AND TUG-O-WAR ARE
TWO WAYS WE USE OUR
BICEPS MUSCLES WHEN WE PLAY.

Our forearm muscles are used every day. How do we use our forearm muscles? These muscles are used for twisting and turning movements.

Our fingers and forearms hold our pencils in place. Writing a note, finishing homework, or doing a few pushups recruits our forearm muscles.

The forearm muscles are located just below your arms or wrists. Can you locate your forearm muscles? Our forearm muscles are used for play! Gripping a bat during a game of baseball or softball is just one way we use our forearm muscles for play.

Did you know there are five muscles in our foot? Just under the skin on your foot you can find those muscles. Try wiggling all five muscles or playing a game of freeze tag! Just another way we use our muscles everyday!

We also use our calf muscles every day! The calf muscles support us while we stand and even while we sit in our seat. Sitting and standing are just two ways we use our calf muscles every day.

The calf muscles are located just above the heel of your foot. Can you locate your calf muscles?

We can also use our calf muscles for play!
Jumping and sprinting in a game of basketball or
dodge ball are just two ways we use our calf
muscles during play.

The quadriceps muscles are located just above the knee. We can use our quadriceps muscles for play! We use our quadriceps for climbing, dancing, galloping, and skipping during play.

Our hamstrings muscles are also used just about every day. For many of us, these muscles are used for pushing movements every day. We might also use these muscles to stop in place or wait in line. Can you think of other ways we use our hamstring muscles every day?

_____

_____

The hamstring muscles are located just above your calf muscles. We can also use our hamstring muscles for play! Our hamstring muscles are used for quick and sudden stops. Engaging in games like Red Light, Green Light, or Freeze Tag are two ways we use our hamstring muscles while playing.

THE CATZ IN T-TYME

HOW DO WE USE OUR MUSCLES EVERYDAY

THE MUSCLES IN OUR CHEST
ARE USED EVERYDAY.
OUR CHEST KEEPS OUR HEART
AND LUNGS PROTECTED.
THE STEADY BEAT OF OUR
HEART HELPS TO KEEP US ALIVE.

OUR LUNGS HOLD THE AIR THAT WE TAKE IN
THROUGH OUR NOSE AND MOUTH.
WE ALSO USE THE MUSCLES
IN OUR CHEST FOR PLAY!
A GAME OF SOCCER IS JUST ONE WAY WE USE
OUR CHEST MUSCLES FOR PLAY.
CAN YOU THINK OF ANOTHER WAY
WE USE OUR CHEST MUSCLES DURING PLAY?

We also use our shoulder muscles every day! Just above your triceps and biceps muscles are your shoulders! The shoulder can carry a huge load of weight. An example of how we use our shoulder muscles at play is cheering on the home team in a competitive game of football! Can you think of other ways we use our shoulder muscles every day?

_____
_____
_____

Class, what have we learnt or found truly interesting today?

Ms Tisbit, to me, it's just interesting just how much we use our muscles every day!

I agree with you, Todd. We rely heavily on our muscles. That's why it's so important to take care of our muscles in every way possible.

HOW DO WE USE OUR MUSCLES EVERYDAY

We also use our shoulder muscles every day! Just above your triceps and biceps muscles are your shoulders! The shoulder can carry a huge load of weight. An example of how we use our shoulder muscles at play is cheering on the home team in a competitive game of football! Can you think of other ways we use our shoulder muscles every day?

THE CATZ IN T-TYME

MA THEMA'S FITNESS BREAK "AQUA FITNESS"

1. AQUA AEROBICS

2. AQUA YOGA

3. AQUA WALKING

4. TAI CHI

Yunias,

Thank you for the many years of tireless work, spectacular drawings and commitment fulfilling my vision of having a wonderful comic strip, Yunias, you are very talented, humble and blessed. I wish you and your family continued success and blessings.

Blessings Omar

THE CATZ

"HERO" CHARACTER CHART

TERRY

TINA

TODD

TABBY

THAD

TIA

THE CATZ

"VILLAIN" CHARACTER CHART

QUEEN TULA

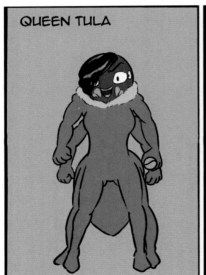

KING TURO

TAP

TURMIT

SABORFOSSIL

SCOREION

THE CATZ IN T-TYME
LITERACY LESSONS

Pre-K/Kindergarten

Pre-K Intentional Read Aloud The Catz In T-Tyme

Lesson Objective: Children will begin to understand that some text contains information.

Lesson Materials: *The Catz In T-Tyme*, Body Builder Picture

Pre-Reading Focus Activity: Show the children a picture of a body builder and ask: Does this person have BIG muscles or small muscles? Do you think they're strong? How do you think their muscles got so BIG and strong? Have the children flex their arm muscles.

Before Reading: Introduce the book (author, illustrator, title, cover, spine). The title of this book is *The Catz In T-Tyme.*

Take a good look at the front cover. What do you think this book is about? How do you know that?

During Reading:

Encourage children to point to their abdominal muscles. (Page 3) Encourage children to point to their bicep muscles. (Page 5) Encourage children to point to their calve muscles. (Page 7) Encourage children to point to their chests. (Page 9)

Encourage children to point to their forearm muscles. (Page 10)

Encourage children to point to their quadriceps muscles. (Page 11) Encourage children to point to their hamstring muscles. (Page 12) Encourage children to point to their shoulders and shrug them. (Page 13)

After Reading:

Did the characters in the book move around a lot or sit still? What were some of the activities the characters did to keep their muscles healthy and strong?

Is moving our muscles a healthy way to make our muscles strong? What are some other ways we can make our muscles healthy and strong?

Who can point to one muscle on their body that we read about today in the book?

Follow Up Activities:

*BIG and Strong Muscles Collage:

Using magazine clippings, create a classroom collage of people exercising, stretching, and eating healthy.

*Create a classroom book:

Take pictures of the children using their muscles in various ways and put them together in a binder for the classroom library. Children can also take turns bringing the book home to share with their families.

Kindergarten Intentional Read Aloud The Catz In T-Tyme

Lesson Objective and Rationale:

*How to find key details in a text.

*Good readers are able to find the key details in a book. It helps them to better comprehend it.

Preview Targeted Learning Behaviors:

*Sitting with pretzel legs

*Look and listen to the speaker

Lesson Materials:

The Catz In T-Tyme, chart paper

Preview Targeted Vocabulary:

muscle: a body tissue that can contract and produce movement (http://www.learnersdictionary.com/defintion/muscle)

abdominal: stomach bicep: upper arm calve:

lower leg forearm: lower arm

fact: something that is true that we need to know

When students hear a vocabulary word during the reading they can give a thumbs up or flex their biceps.

Before Reading:

Readers, today we are going to read a nonfiction text about the muscles in our bodies called The Catz In T-Tyme. While we read we are going to focus on one key detail. A key detail in nonfiction is the facts the book is teaching us. Facts are true statements that we need to know about.

Introduce Targeted Vocabulary During Reading:

Preview the front and back covers, the spine and discuss the author, illustrator and the title.

Talking Points:

*What are the characters doing on the front cover? I wonder why they're doing that?

*Can you believe we have nearly 630 muscles in our bodies? (Page 2)

*Discuss the different actions the characters are doing throughout the book.

-swing

-walk

-bend

-run

-jump

-bounce

-kick ,dance

After Reading:

What was the title of the book?

What was the main topic the book talked about? (Muscles, different ways to move our muscles)

Who can name one muscle we learned about today? Who can show me different ways to move their muscles?

What were some of the actions the characters did with their muscles? Why is it important for us to move our muscles?

What do you think would happen if we didn't move our muscles?

Follow Up Activity:

On chart paper, make a class list of the different actions people do with their muscles and perform them.

Kindergarten Writing Lesson *The Catz In T-Tyme*

Lesson Objective and Rationale:

*How to draw a picture on one specific topic.

*Good writers are able to choose a topic and write or draw a picture to go with it. It helps them to get their ideas across clearly.

Preview Targeted Learning Behaviors:

*Look and listen to the speaker

*Follow the directions given to complete the drawing and the sentences.

Lesson Materials:

*The Catz In T-Tyme

*Action Words Class List onchart paper *My Muscles And MeWorksheets

Before Writing:

Writers, today we are going to learn to draw a picture on one specific topic. Our topic is My Muscles And Me. Just like the characters in, *The Catz In T-Tyme*, we are going to think of an action we do with our muscles, draw a picture of it and write the word.

Display the Action Words List created during the follow-up activity. Encourage the children to choose one action they can do with their muscles and draw a picture of it.

Preview the My Muscles And Me worksheet template and distribute.

During Writing:

Refer to the Action Words List and encourage children to write the action they chose on the correct line.

After Writing:

Remember, today we learned how to draw a picture on one topic, actions we can do with our muscles. Good writers pay attention to the topic and follow the directions because it helps them to get their ideas across clearly.

My Muscles And Me

My name is _____

I have lots of muscles.

I can _____ with my muscles.

THE CATZ IN T-TYME

MATH LESSONS

Pre-K/Kindergarten

Pre-K/Kindergarten Math Activity The Catz In T-Tyme

Count With Whole Numbers

Lesson Objective: Children will use rote-counting skills to count to 20 by ones.

Materials: Multiple six-sided dice with dots or numbers pre-written on them, The Catz In T-Tyme

Activity: Large or Small Groups

Assemble children in a group and ask them to spread out. Show the children The Catz In T-Tyme and explain that they will exercise just like the characters in the book.

Show the children the dice and explain to them that dice have numbers/dots on them. "Today we will roll the dice, observe the number shown, then perform different actions with our bodies the number of times the dice says." Be sure to count aloud during the action.

Different actions to perform:

jumping-jacks arm circles jumping

hopping on one foot jogging in place sit-ups push- ups

Variations:

*Use Flash Cards with numbers instead of dice.
Children can draw a card, identity the number, and then everyone can join in performing an action.

*Children can think of a number from 1-20 then perform the action the correct number of times.

*Make a class list of different actions the children can perform and count how many there are.

*Children can draw a card and bounce a ball or jump rope according to the number shown.

When the children have completed the actions, discuss how some of their actions were the same as the characters in the book.

Page 2: The termite, Turnit, does **sit-ups**. Page 3: The little cat, Todd, does **sit-ups**. Page 5: The cat, Tabby, **jumped** with a rope. Page 7: The big cat, Thad, **bounced** a ball.

Page 9: The little cat, Todd, does **push-ups**.

Discuss which muscles the children used to complete each action.

Pre-K/Kindergarten Math Activity The Catz In T-Tyme

Obstacle Course

Lesson Objective: Children will understand the spatial concepts of over, under, across, through, and around.

Materials: table, jump rope, tunnel, scooter, chair

Activity: Large or Small Group

Assemble the children and ask them to sit with "pretzel" legs (crisscross-applesauce). Show the children The Catz In T-Tyme and explain that they will exercise just like the characters in the book.

*Note: To reinforce listening skills and promote good- sportsmanship have the children repeat the directions aloud, complete the obstacle course one at a time, and cheer for each other.

Explain that each child will complete the obstacle course by:

*crawling **under** a table

*riding a scooter **across** the floor

*jumping **over** a jump rope (two children can hold the ends and wiggle the rope on the floor)

*crawling **through** a tunnel

*walking **around** a chair

*sitting back down in their spot

When each child has completed the obstacle course, discuss how some of their actions were the same as the characters in the book. Page 1: The little cat, Todd, pulled his baby cousins in the wagon **across** the playground.

Page 1: Tabby pushes the little cat, Todd, **through** the air on the swing.

Page 8: The three catz, Todd, Terry and Tina swung the bats **around** their bodies.

Discuss which muscles the children used to complete the obstacle course.

Kindergarten Math Activity The Catz In T-Tyme

Musical Chairs

Operations and Algebraic Thinking

Lesson Objective and Rationale:

Children will be able to solve simple subtraction problems within 10. Mathematicians are able to add and subtract within 10. Lesson Materials: chairs, music, The Catz In T-Tyme

Preview Targeted Learning Behaviors:

*Look and listen to the speaker

*Follow the directions given the first time

Before Playing:

Mathematicians, today we will play a game involving subtraction. Subtraction means

taking numbers apart or making them smaller. Good mathematicians can subtract. It helps them better understand how many objects are in a group.

Hold up 5 fingers then point to and count each one. Fold one finger down. Ask the children how many are left. "I subtracted one finger and made the number smaller. I had 5 but now I have 4. 4 is smaller than 5."

Show the children The Catz In T-Tyme and point out how some characters in the book danced to music. We will do subtraction today by playing musical chairs.

When we start the game, there will be 10 chairs in a line.10 students will walk around the chairs while music is playing. When the music stops, everyone must sit down in a chair.

Each time the music starts again I will take away one chair, which means there will be a smaller number of chairs and more children.

If you can't find a chair when the music stops your time playing the game is over.

*Note: To continue the lesson, place number cards from 1-10 on a table. As each child leaves the game, they can take the next number in the sequence and stand in line in numerical order.

Play The Game:

Model for children how to walk around and sit safely on the chairs.

After Playing:

When the game is over discuss how some of the children's actions were the same as the characters in the book.

Page 10: The catz, Terry and Tina, danced.

Page 11: The smallest cat, Todd, leads the way in a game of follow the leader.

Complimentary Songs

Thank you for your purchase! To enjoy a complimentary download of the songs for this book Our Muscles Are Used Everyday visit our roku channel, Tenacious Fitness Unlimited, Inc. or go to www.tfitu.com

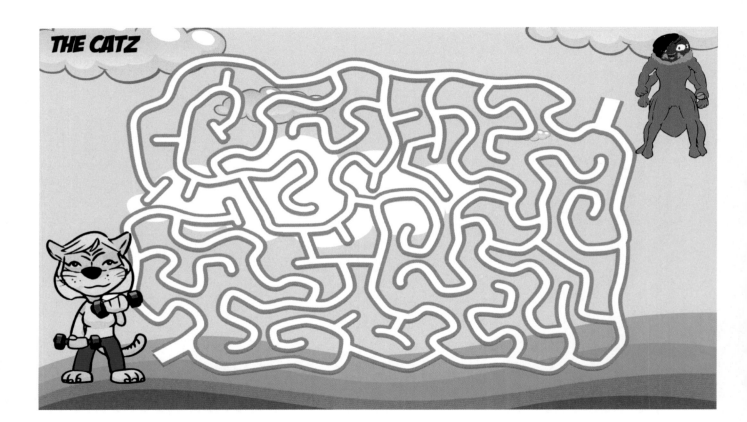

Made in the USA
Middletown, DE
27 April 2022

64865277R00031